Kishkindhya Kand

Kishkindhya Kand

(A romantic murder mystery in the backdrop of historical Hampi)

Ananya Pal

Hornbill Press

ISBN-13: 9789387885646

Cover design by: Anindita Dutta

Printed in the United States of America & in India

I owe all my creative endeavours to the creator
of the Universe;
I connect with him through my writing.
Bless me my Lord to be honest with myself,
Bless me to be worthy of your blessings.

Anindita, this novel is dedicated to our friendship and the marvellous trip to Hampi together

and

also, to the adorable young guide Maruti who added special essence to our experiences there.

Author's note

Four years ago, during one of my frequent visits to Kolkata, Anindita and I were having an idle discussion over coffee. Suddenly, the idea of another historical vacation came up, this time within India. Our previous trip together to Myanmar a few months earlier made us hungry for some more adventure. It was Anindita who suggested a trip to the Hampi belt and also made the necessary arrangements. I was living in Dhaka at that time. The seven-day tour to Hampi, Badami, Pattadakal, Aihole and Mysore surpassed my expectations and remained preserved in the treasure trove of my memory.

I usually pen down all my travel experiences, but this trip became one of the exceptions, since I was sucked up in my professional commitments immediately on return. I regretted not writing down my experiences for a long time, till I finally decided to turn this experience into a story, on an impulse.

This novel is a work of fiction, but our amazing travel experience remains entwined in it. That is why the storyline, though primarily a murder mystery, reflects a tour to this amazing region of historical sites.

I thank my publisher Arunava Chatterjee for believing in me and also the editor Romila Sundaresan for giving the finer touches to my writing.

Ananya Pal

Prologue

Rudrapur is a city in Udham Singh Nagar District, Uttarakhand; about 250 km. from both Delhi and Dehradun. The settlement was developed in the 1960s; most of the population at that time represented migrants from both Pakistan and World War II torn Burma. In the last thirty years, that once sleepy town has emerged as a flourishing agricultural and industrial city.

The Tarai region boasts immense bounty of nature, both in terms of panoramic views and agricultural produce, especially fruits and herbs. There are a few food processing units running successfully in the city, one of the most successful being Deb Food Products. As a private limited company, owned by the Deb family, it has managed to sail through time, while exploring new opportunities. Their new unit, opened in recent years, specialises in vacuum dried fruits, flowers and herbs; though the regulars like food preserve, jams and pickles still continue to be the flagship products. They also have retail outlets in and aroundRudrapur.

The Deb family was among the early settlers in the city. The late patriarch of the family, Jagmohan Deb, a Bengali timber merchant in British Burma, had to flee the country during the World War II bombing, with his wife and a toddler son, leaving behind his fortune. Since then, his journey via Northeast India to Kolkata and ultimately to Rudrapur was a story of hardship and determination that had taken the form of a legend within the family over time. The foundation of this current day business was laid by him, with a humble start based on the capital earned by selling his wife's jewellery. All this happened a long time ago. Today, the impressive bungalow of the family, "Debalay," is the pride of the posh society of Amravati Colony and reflects the success story of Jagmohan's son, Sudhamoy Deb, and in recent years, of the son's wife, Ambika Deb.

Ambika was Sudhamoy's second wife. His first wife, Tripti, had died young, leaving behind a son, aged only two. It was rumoured that the marriage hadn't been a success. The couple remained childless for nine years, while Tripti lapsed in and out of depression during this period. She finally, almost miraculously conceived and delivered a son, but never got back to her jovial self again. Ambika Mitra, daughter of a local school master, joined Deb Food Products as a shorthand typist and in no time became Sudhamoy's personal assistant, due to her dedication and sharp mind. It was during that phase that Tripti died of a freak accident at home.

On a Sunday afternoon, Sudhamoy was cleaning his licensed rifle, Tripti was sitting next to him; it was their usual evening teatime. The rifle accidentally fired during the cleaning process and Tripti was shot. She was rushed to the local hospital first and then to Delhi, but all was in vain. Tripti died in a coma after a month. Ambika took charge of the shattered household during this time of grief, as there was no one else in the family. She took the helpless child, Bikram, under her wing; Sudhamoy was charged with the murder of his wife. He was out on bail after a couple of days, but the legal procedure became lengthy and traumatic. Ultimately, he was acquitted by the lower court due to lack of direct evidence and no one appealed further.

He was acquitted by a court of justice, but not by society. Hushed rumours and a sense of discomfort prevailed at parties and at the club, whenever he was around. It made him gradually withdraw from the world and shut himself into a cocoon of work, work, work. Again, Ambika came as a great support; she stood by him like a stalwart. In a few months' time they got married; the Deb household fell in place; Bikram found a mother and Sudhamoy was happy in this marriage like never. Eventually, they were blessed with one more son, Avijit, and a daughter, Nandini.

Ambika proved to be an ideal partner, not only in personal life, but in professional life too. She continued taking part in the business affairs of Deb Food Products and Sudhamoy was grateful for that.

Sudhamoy wasn't destined to enjoy marital bliss much longer. He departed the world after fighting a prolonged battle with cancer in just ten years of their marriage; he was only 53 and all his children minors. Ambika was named the sole beneficiary in his will.

Bikram, bookish and an introvert, wanted to study history, but did a Masters in Agricultural Economics instead, from Govind Ballabh Pant University of Agriculture, on Ambika's insistence. Soon after graduating, he joined his mother to take care of the family business.

Avijit grew up a little bratty, probably as an outcome of the only weakness in Ambika's character. He went to study in Delhi University, stayed there for 5 years; even managed to earn a degree in Commerce, but came back home reluctantly, with no real ambition in life. He hardly took any interest in the business, though never denied the wealth and luxury that it bestowed on him. Ambika, true to her character, restricted the flow of funds to him, with the condition that he needed to attend office and married him off to a bright young Bengali girl from Kolkata. She expected Shrirupa, her daughter-in-law, to oversee his life and it happened exactly the way Ambika desired, under her close supervision, of course.

Nandini, a sweet-natured girl, neither inherited her mother's wit, nor her character; Ambika got a sense of that quite early. As a result, a marriage was arranged for Nandini while she was still in high school to the only son of Sunil Verma, a local wealthy businessman. The marriage couldn't sustain the stress of constant ego clashes between the formidable Sunil Verma and the interfering Ambika. In just three years, Ankit and Nandini separated; she came back to her mother with an infant daughter, Tiara. The divorce was filed and Ambika didn't allow Nandini to claim alimony. In due course, Tiara was admitted in a boarding school in Dehradun, though the battle for custody was still on.

At present, the Deb household runs smoothly; the family business reaching new heights, under Ambika relentless control. Bikram, at 35, was still a bachelor; he spent much of his spare time in his private study, indulging his passion for history. Shrirupa and Avijit were yet to be blessed with a child, though they didn't seem to mind it. Nandini stopped brooding over her failed marriage and was quite active in her social circuit. They all adored Ambika, the driving force in their life.

The rhythm of the household, however, received a jolt when Ambika suffered a sudden stroke a year ago. She was left with a heart condition and a weak left leg. Although Ambika might have become frail in health, her spirit was as vigorous as ever. She ran her office from home and lately even started attending the office once a week, much to the surprise of the doctors. Uma, a distant relative from Delhi and a qualified nurse, came to take care of Ambika in the initial months of the crisis and stayed on with the family on her insistence.

***

Chapter 1

Amaravati Colony, Rudrapur

The corner house faced the park. An otherwise imposing structure, it was eclipsed in the timid glow from a lamppost near the park gate. In the sleepy moonless night of winter, the house remained quiet, almost melancholic, with no signs of life apparent from its shroud of darkness.

Yet, there was a sliver of light that escaped through the crack of a slightly ajar door of a small anteroom in the eastern corner. This was the private study of Bikram, his preferred refuge in this large house. He was totally engrossed, magnifying glass in hand, peering at a map of medieval India, laid out on the table. As Bikram leaned in to see the tiny details on the map, the table-lamp highlighted his fine features, stubble and thick longish hair. At thirty-five, he was unnervingly handsome. These aquiline features were probably the only heritage left to him by his late mother. A slight buck tooth did show up whenever he smiled and his intelligent eyes expressed empathy. Though the most attractive part was that he was completely unaware of all this.

"Bikram da, your coffee," a young woman in her late twenties entered with a tray in hand.

"Why did you bother Uma? It's already so late!" Bikram's voice was refined and melodious.

"I was awakeanyway, Masi needed to use the toilet."

"You spoil me with so much attention, what will happen when you leave?" he teased her smilingly. There was genuine gratitude in his voice.

Her face lit up. Such appreciation from an otherwise quiet man meant a lot. She looked at his face, probably in search of something more, her eyes betrayed her feelings; but he had already gone back to studying the map. She lingered for a moment and then left, softly closing the door behind her.

After a while, someone tried the main door with a key. It needed a few attempts and some hushed instructions. Two shadows entered the hall and tiptoed towards a first-floor bedroom. The clanking of the colony watchman's baton on the road outside resonated in the deep silence. It was two in the morning.

"You shouldn't drink more than you can handle, how many times do I need to remind you Avijit?" Shrirupa reacted under her breath, as her husband collapsed on the bed, fully dressed. Her words didn't reach his ears; he had already passed out.

Shrirupa took time to change and remove her make up. An attractive woman with intelligent eyes and a determined chin looked back at her in the mirror. A sigh escaped her lips, as she pondered over her image for a moment and then moved towards the bed. She gently took off Avijit's shoes and pulled a blanket on him, her fingers brushed the unruly curls from his forehead almost mechanically, before putting off the bedside lamp.

A mass of darkness gathered around another windowpane, with a young face silhouetted in the silver lining of the lamppost's light. Nandini looked vulnerable, lost in thought. Another sleepless night it was, a nice dose of sleeping pills was too alluring at this moment to take care of that persistent pain of spondylitis, or was it something else?

***

The spacious library at the back of the hallway showcased a fine collection of books, both in English and Bengali. They ranged from the classics to the contemporary, literature, philosophy and even theology. Sudhamoy had been an avid reader all his life, though the current generation didn't seem to harbour the same interest, except Bikram. Ever since Ambika had fallen ill, this room had been converted into her office. Despite her frail health, she was still a formidable figure, towering over the large desk with her penetrating gaze and defined jawline. She had greyed far more than her actual years; the lines on her face were the relics of hard-work and authority, rather than advancing age. There were files stacked neatly on the desk for her consideration; her secretary Piyush helped her with the papers. A laptop was lying open at her side, though it wasn't her preferred tool.

"Madam, Bikram Sir asked me to remind you about the new Greenhouse project file."

"That's alright; I need to discuss it with Mr. Khanna. When is he coming?"

"He is on his way, he messaged."

"Did you inform Avijit to attend the meeting too?"

"Yes, Madam," said Piyush, with a slight hesitation in his voice.

"Is he not coming with Mr. Khanna?" Ambika was sharp to sense it.

"Actually, Avijit Sir isn't in office today."

"Uma!" she barked from her desk, while pressing the calling bell. Uma rushed in from the hallway.

"Ask Shrirupa if Avijit has left for office."

Uma seemed to hesitate a few seconds before answering, "Dada is working from home today, Boudi said he has fever."

"I see. Have you checked on him and suggested some medicine?"

"Boudi has."

"OK then," Ambika dismissed Uma with a motion of her hand.

"Shrirupa, send him to the library, tell him Mr. Khanna is on his way," Ambika's voice was stern on the mobile.

'Ma, actually...''

"Now, don't give me that age-old excuse of fever! If I can work, he can work too. Let me make one thing very clear to both of you: if he wants his Pantnagar project to be approved, he must try very hard." This time her voice was icy, as she ended the call.

Mr. Khanna, the trusted General Manager of too many years to count, had already attained retirement age, though his appearance spoke otherwise. Ambika had no intention of letting him go and had gotten his extension approved by the board recently. Khanna was a man of few words, a quiet yet amiable personality that often balanced the authoritative character of Ambika in the office.

"What do you think about this Pantnagar project Mr. Khanna?"

"The realty business is booming in Uddham Singh Nagar no doubt; the land is in a strategic location too," Mr. Khanna spoke slowly.

"So, should we go ahead with it? Diversity is a good strategy in today's competitive market, isn't it?"

"Yes, of course. But, if we try for bank funding for both the Pantnagar project and that Bazipur Greenhouse, it will be difficult."

"Do you suggest we take up only one of them at this moment to avoid over exposure?"

"Exactly. The proposed new greenhouse in Bazipur would mean product diversification with measured risk. Bikram is a responsible boy; he has thought through all the possibilities."

"So, you are in favour of Greenhouse, rather than the Pantnagar Housing Project?"

"There are a few factors to be considered regarding the Pantnagar project. Firstly, a new company has to be opened, as the line of business is different. Then, if we go by Avijit's suggestion, his friend Aneesh would be a shareholder; the first one outside the Deb family. Above all, Avijit doesn't have any previous experience in this line of business."

"But there is always a first time for everything Khanna ji."

"Oh, yes. I'm sure Madam, he will do well," Khanna was quick to pick up the trail.

Ambika was about to send for Avijit when he entered the library in quite a dishevelled state. He pulled a chair to sit beside Mr. Khanna; there was a certain earnestness in his attitude.

"We were discussing about your project," Ambika resumed the conversation.

"So, what has been decided?" Avijit retorted.

"There are certain factors to be discussed before taking any decision Avijit, you must understand," Ambika answered.

"So much of discussion for a few crores! My friend won't wait for eternity, neither will the land owner."

"What would be the ratio of shareholding – between you and Aneesh I mean."

"The capital will be mine; I've already clarified this with Khanna Uncle, but profit sharing will be equal, so naturally shareholding will be equal."

"Don't you think, it would be better if you take Aneesh as the CEO and may be also a director, but not as a shareholder? You and Shrirupa can become two shareholders instead," Ambika tried to persuade.

"That's preposterous! It's Aneesh's brainchild, he is a civil engineer, works as a PWD contractor."

"Khanna Ji what do you suggest?"

The veteran employee took some time and then made a suggestion. "In that case Madam, the fund would float from Deb Food Products as a loan and there would be representation on the board from it."

"Oh yes, that's settled then. Khanna ji and I will be on the board, Khanna ji will oversee the business affairs, as he does for Deb Food Products," Ambika stated decisively.

It was clear from her tone that the decision wasn't negotiable. Avijit didn't look too pleased, but kept quiet, sensing the situation.

***

Dinner time at the Deb household was at 7.30 in the evening, quite early by Indian standards. Ambika was very particular about maintaining the time. On her insistence, everyone gathered around for dinner, unless out on an urgent commitment. The menu usually was an elaborate affair, catering to individual tastes. Ambika ensured that too. Till date, the cook took her advice to decide on meals; Shrirupa had hardly any say in it. Everyone would gather around in the first-floor lounge for some family time post dinner; that was also a part of the dinner ritual.

It was during this post dinner family time that Ambika told Bikram that his proposal had been shelved for the time being.

"Your brother's project needed immediate funds; the landowner has other offers."

"Yes, I understand." Bikram was a bit jolted but recovered quickly.

"My greenhouse proposal is shelved, but what about the holiday proposal," he smiled at his mother most disarmingly.

The family went for an annual holiday together, every winter around Christmas, and Bikram usually coordinated this trip. Earlier, it used to be a foreign destination, but keeping in mind Ambika's health condition, this year they decided to holiday in South India, around Bangalore. Ambika didn't want to travel by air and South India would provide respite from the bitter cold of Uttarakhand.

Bikram wanted to visit the architectural marvels of the Vijayangara Kingdom, while the ladies wanted to shop in Mysore. So, the itinerary was carefully chalked out. It would be Rudrapur to Delhi by car and then the rest of the journey by train, taking the route Delhi to Bangalore, Bangalore to Mysore and then to Hampi, and from there back to Bangalore and Delhi. It was to be a leisurely trip of two weeks, where the longest stay would be in Hampi, for eight days. That way, Ambika would get enough rest and they could cover all the historical sites of the region, which included Hampi, Badami, Aiholc and Pattadakal.

Everyone started participating in the holiday plan enthusiastically; all except Avijit. He never showed much interest in family matters, though didn't object either. Ambika immensely enjoyed such conversations, where she remained the nucleus; it gave her a sense of fulfilment.

*** ***

Chapter 2

It was the Bangalore City Junction railway station. The Hampi Express arrived at Platform No. 1 at 21.55 hours sharp, as per schedule. The platform wasn't too crowded and there wasn't much of a rush near the air-conditioned compartments. Two young women in their early thirties hurried towards the first-class AC coach, one of them scoured the reservation list for "Meghna Sen" and "Aditi Datta." Satisfied to have found the names, she allowed herself to be shepherded in by the coolie carrying their luggage. It took a while to fit in all the luggage and settle down on their designated berths. It was a four-berth cabin.

"The coach has one more four berth cabin and two twin-berth ones. Is this your first time to Hampi, Madam?"

"How do you know we are going to Hampi?"

"You look like tourists; all the tourists go to Hampi on this train."

The cabin attendant was chatty, with good sense of humour, the ladies noticed while he handed over the fresh bedlinen and towels.

As they settled down on their allotted berths, one of them took stock of the cabin.

"It's quite comfortable, kind of private. I'm quite thrilled." The speaker was a chirpy young woman, with an easy manner and pretty face that reflected an innocent charm. Her companion gave an indulging smile; she was a very attractive woman, with an intelligent face, large eyes and a long braid to go with her tall frame. She was the more reserved of the two, with an imposing personality. Two made for an interesting pair.

Meghna, the chirpy one, was a lecturer in a business school in Kolkata and a freelance writer; a detective story writer to be precise. She had recently had a book published too, which was doing well, to her own surprise. Aditi was a doctor attached to a reputed private hospital in the City of Joy and an ace photographer. Her love for photography and Meghna's natural curiosity towards romantic thrills often brought them to visit various historical sites. Meghna was married, with an absentee husband, who was mostly on business tours abroad. Aditi was still single; both were fiercely independent and fond of travelling, especially to the places lesser travelled by conventional tourists; hence the choice of Hampi.

There was another occupant of the cabin, an elderly lady. She had clearly boarded the train much earlier, probably at Mysore.

"The fourth berth still remains vacant, that means we can't lock the cabin door yet," the older lady showed her displeasure as the train was about to move.

She was in her sixties, elegant and well-dressed, although a bit aloof in her attitude, which often resulted from holding a position of power. The younger duo acknowledged her with a smile.

"Maybe it will remain vacant," Meghna suggested.

"I doubt it. I saw a gentleman's name in the list," the lady replied.

"I am Aditi, and this is Meghna," Aditi introduced themselves out of politeness and maybe to divert the discussion too. In response, the lady gave her own introduction. She was Mrs. Sunita Sethi from Delhi and as her personality suggested, was a retired principal of a reputed school in South Delhi. She had also been a valuable member of the educational board for several years. Today, she was travelling alone.

At that moment, the attendant ushered in a gentleman of medium height and salt and pepper hair; he was wearing a blue jacket and grey trouser.

"That's your seat sir," the attendant indicated towards the empty upper berth, while providing the bed linen. The gentleman, a bit confused, put down his kit bag and followed the attendant out of the cabin.

"It can't be mine," he whispered to the attendant. He was speaking in Hindi and it was evident that he had no command over the language.

"Why Sir, check your ticket."

"It's a ladies' compartment."

"No Sir, there isn't any Ladies-only cabin in 1st class."

"But please shift me to another cabin," the man was visibly nervous.

"That's not possible Sir, other cabins are all full. A large family is travelling together in two other cabins and the last twin is occupied by a *phirangi* (European) couple. No one will switch seats with you."

"Then, do you want me to sleep with the ladies?" This time he shouted at the attendant irritably.

"No Sir, why with the ladies? You sleep on your own berth," the staff remarked with an impish smirk on his face, as the train started off with a lurch.

The man came back inside the cabin, clearly resigned to his fate. Meghna was thoroughly enjoying the situation and this time she took charge.

"Hi! I am Meghna Sen from Kolkata."

"You are Bengali!" the man had instinctively switched to Bengali in his excitement. His accent wasn't that of Kolkata though; it carried the flavour from beyond the border.

In another ten minutes, the circumstances changed quite dramatically. He not only gave his details but turned out to be an amiable and pleasant character in the process. Sukhdev Saha was a businessman from Bangladesh.

"My son refused to take interest in the family business; we have been into Jute for three generations. Niloy is a software engineer, he studied in the US and joined an MNC there. He was sent to Bangalore for a year on deputation last August," Sukhdev explained, while informing them that he had come to visit his son and, on his insistence, had taken this trip to Hampi. Sukhdev was a widower.

***

"Excuse me, you dropped this," Aditi looked back at the refined voice in the passageway. She saw a young man holding her watch; it must have slipped out of her wrist while returning from the toilet. She had noticed him talking to the attendant earlier; now she took a closer look. The stranger was really very attractive, even for her snobbish taste.

"Thank you," she responded, with a polite smile.

"Sir, there isn't any pantry on this train; can't get you hot water," the attendant intervened.

"What happened? Why do you need hot water?" Aditi enquired.

"Actually, my mother has a backache; a hot water bag would have been a relief."

"I have some hot patches, they can help; should I get them for you?" she offered.

"Oh, that would be wonderful! By the way I am Bikram."

"I am Aditi." Bikram came to their cabin to take the patches and looked visibly impressed by her cordiality and maybe something more.

"Isn't he handsome?" Meghna whispered in her typicaleagerness, as Bikram left. Aditi frowned at her irritably.

***

The Deb family was engrossed in the bigger cabin with small talk when Bikram handed over the patches. He explained the use of it and left for the next cabin. Uma immediately got on the job of putting them on Ambika; Shrirupa and Nandini got back to their discussion. Avijit sat in a corner, quite motionless; the surroundings didn't seem to bother him in any way at all. After a while, as the pain eased, Ambika asked Shrirupa to take out some sweets and distribute them.

"It was an early dinner; everyone must be hungry," she quipped.

It was Mysore Paak, bought in Mysore, as a family favourite. Everyone was enjoying the sweets, even Ambika took a bite, but Avijit refused. He even snubbed Shrirupa when she insisted. The mood in the cabin turned sombre suddenly. Uma quietly took a portion and left.

"Bikram da, some Mysore Paak for you," Bikram looked up from the book he was reading. There was softness in his expression as he accepted the sweet.

"Have you eaten?" he asked.

"Now I shall," she smiled shyly and left.

***

The train reached Hospet station at 7.10 am, it was a misty winter morning; the platform was busy with coolies and expectant auto rickshaw drivers, running around to attract customers. There was queue at the doorway of the first-class AC coach, with travellers waiting to get off the train, which stopped for only five minutes here. The Deb family occupied the entire front exit space, so the rest of the passengers had lined up at the back door. Mrs. Sethi was the last one in the queue, with a suitcase and a cabin bag to manage. She was a bit nervous, as the whistle blew.

"Madam, please get down quickly. I'll take care of the luggage," Sukhdev Saha grabbed her luggage, while ushering the dazed lady out; not caring about his own luggage lying unattended on the platform. She couldn't thank him enough for such unexpected chivalry. A cab driver came forward with a placard that had her name on it. Sukhdev, unsure of what to do next, moved forward to find an auto rickshaw.

"I can give you a lift Mr. Saha," she came forward, as Sukhdev was trying to negotiate with a driver; his Hindi wasn't helping much in the process.

"No need Madam, please don't bother." He seemed a bit taken aback with the kind offer from such an aloof lady.

"Trust me, it's no trouble. It would be a pleasure."

"But I am booked in Hotel Ambassador, would it be on your way?" He was still hesitant.

"Oh! That would be very convenient. I am booked there too," she smiled and took the lead, following the cab driver.

The Deb family were seen getting into a pre-booked SUV outside the station gates; their destination was Hotel Ambassador too. That wasn't a surprise at all. Ambassador was the only Star hotel in Hampi.

"How much will it be for Hotel Ambassador?" Meghna took charge while negotiating with an auto rickshaw driver. The man was very young, clearly in his early twenties. He was tall, dark, with large, expressive eyes, thick longish hair, and a moustache to go with it. He would have fitted well in the backdrop of the historical sites, Meghnaconsidered. There was earnestness in his manner, which was why they had gravitated to him over the others.

"Give me whatever you think fit Madam, let me take you to the parking."

"We can't do that. You must quote a price," Meghna insisted.

"Madam, I will take you to all the tourist sites around here. Keep my mobile number," he evaded the topic of price.

On Aditi's nod, Meghna agreed, and they proceeded to the parking.

"Is it your first time here Madam?" The auto driver started a conversation while driving.

"Yes."

"How long do you plan to stay here?"

"A week."

"Then you must visit Badami caves too. For that you will require a car. But don't worry, my boss has cars too."

"You have a boss?"

"Yes Madam, I drive his auto, it isn't mine."

They reached the hotel within what seemed a very short while, with all this conversation.

"Call me when you are ready to explore the city, here's my number." He wrote his mobile number on a piece of paper from a pocket notebook and handed it over.

"What do we call you?" Meghna asked.

"Maruti; I am Maruti, Madam," he smiled most endearingly, and his face lit up with it.

"My name is Meghna, and she is Aditi," Meghna responded while parting.

"See you soon Madam," he called out from behind.

*** ***

Chapter 3

The Ambassador Hotel was conveniently located at Kamalapur Road, near the Archaeological Museum. Unlike the usual star hotels, it carried a simple elegance, the staff was polite and helpful; overall, the place had a homely atmosphere, despite the underlining professionalism. Meghna and Aditi were the last to arrive at the hotel among the passengers of the AC 1 compartment; the hotel was mostly crowded by tourists from abroad, they noticed.

"Please give us a front facing room," Meghna urged.
"Road facing rooms can be a bit noisy Ma'am, I can provide garden view options."
"We are fine with noise," she persisted; Aditi nudged her discretely, but Meghna remained unperturbed.
"All right Ma'am, a room on the third floor, facing the Museum," the gentleman at the reception handed back their documents with an indulgent smile.

"You're impossible!" Aditi remarked on their way to the room.
"No, I had to do this; people just take it on themselves to decide for the women travellers in India."

"Enough of your feminist lectures. Now that you have the room you desired, let's get ready for the day," Aditi remarked, while going to the bathroom. Meghna went to the window, the beautiful building of the Museum and its lush green lawn came into view; she stood at the window for a long time.

'What's the plan for the day?" Once they were freshened up, Aditi asked Meghna over a cup of black Darjeeling tea. Both of them had a fetish for fine tea; Meghna had remembered to carry a packet of her favourite brand.
"Let's call Maruti post lunch, let him suggest an itinerary for the week. Today we can visit the nearby spots," Meghna responded.
"What time does lunch hour start?"
"I called the reception; it starts at 11.30."
The hotel catered to breakfast, lunch and dinner in buffet system, though there was provision for a-la-carte too. Breakfast was part of the package, but guests could avail any other buffet meal at a fixed charge.
"Great! Then ask Maruti to come at 1.00."

The dining hall was at the ground floor, connected to the lounge through a passageway; it also opened to a lovely garden through a glass door. There was provision for breakfast or evening tea outside, with a few shaded sitting areas. Aditi and Meghna met Mrs. Sethi in the passage; she was also on her way to the dining hall. She smiled at them in acknowledgement and went ahead to sit at a corner table.

"The spread is quite elaborate; I fccl hungry now!" Meghna reacted in her chirpy way.

"Go ahead! Who's stopping you?"

Aditi met Bikram while returning to her table with her plate piled with food. He smiled at her. "Mom felt much better with those patches last night, thanks again. It's a pleasant surprise to meet you here."

"I'm glad to see you too," she responded politely.

"Isn't he the guy from the train last night?"

"Come on, he has a name."

"Of course, he has. Does he have a mobile number too?"

"Will you stop romanticising? He must be married, look at the family," Aditi indicated at the Deb family sitting at a big table on one side of the large dining room.

"Who do you think is the wife?"

"Maybe the smart looking woman, she's attractive."

"Can't be, she's attached to the other man, must be his wife," Meghna remarked; with that their light-hearted gameof guessing continued through lunch.

"Who is she Dadabhai?" Nandini asked Bikram.

"Who; Oh, she's the doctor who helped last night."

"She's very good looking, isn't Shri?" Nadini's comment was meant for Shrirupa, though Ambika responded instead.

"Those two young girls are travelling alone?" It was a remark rather than a question. Bikram shrugged in response.

Bikram proposed a visit to the Virupaksha Temple in the afternoon; that way Ambika could watch the evening aarti too. Ambika snubbed the idea, citing tiredness.

"Yes, of course, I should have realised how tiring the journey must have been for you Ma," he was embarrassed.

"Dadabhai, let's go to the Bazaar Street then, heard a lot about it; Shri and I can do some interesting shopping there," Nandini suggested.

Ambika gestured to Uma to help her get up. As she left the table, the whole family dispersed.

***

The Hazar Rama Temple was located within the royal enclosure of the Deva Raya Dynasty Palace area. The temple had been the place of worship for the royalty during the glorious Vijaynagar Kingdom. Though it was modest in size, in comparison to many others in the city, the beautiful carvings on its walls, depicting the Ramayana and Vishnu Purana, set it apart from the rest. The finely crafted temple pillars suggested the zenith of art and culture that the Kingdom had achieved, apart from its military prowess.

Hampi was very warm even in winter. Meghna and Aditi strolled around enjoying the relics in the cooler atmosphere inside. There weren't many tourists around in this afternoon sun.

"Such marvels!" Aditi remarked, while taking photographs of the pillar carvings.

"Originally built during the 15th century by Devaraya II, though these pillars and relics were added subsequently," Meghna remarked.

"Wow! You have done homework," Aditi teased her.

"I had to; so that you can put nice captions for your pictures on Instagram." They both laughed at that heartily.

They spent much of the afternoon in the temple compound, waiting for the blazing sun to lose some of its ferocity, so that the royal enclosure could be explored, much of which was in the open. The ruins of the ceremonial pavilion, with intricate carvings at the base, had once been an illustrious structure; a massive wooden door lying nearby gave evidence of this fact. There was a public bath and a pond, with beautifully structured geometric steps, meant to be the royal bath in the vicinity. The clean water in the royal bath was too luring in the humid afternoon, Meghna sat on its steps unmindfully; Aditi clicked away at her camera at that scene. The brilliant blue of the sky, the soothing green water and a lone character lost in her own thoughts; she pondered over a suitable caption.

The Queen's Bath was at the other side of the enclave. Maruti took them there in the auto rickshaw; he was doing his best to serve as the guide, even pointing out popular photo spots to Aditi. He was really impressed with her elaborate array of camera and lenses. The Queens' Bath, as expected, was a double storey, enclosed structure, with an open balcony on the first floor, for the ladies-in-waiting. There were beautifully carved fountains at the pillars, meant to pour water to the centre of the artificial tub.

"This is torturous! We are so damn hot and sweaty, just can't enjoy this place as much as I would have liked to," Meghna complained, as Aditi tried to photograph her with a fountain pillar.
"I think we're done for the day, let's go back to the hotel now," Aditi suggested.

***

"Are you game for an exotic Kerala massage?" Meghna nudged Aditi, as she was checking her day's captures. They were duly bathed and rested by now, sitting by the window. It was already dusk. The western horizon over the Museum compound was painted in a riot of colours; in that soft light, the atmosphere in the room was almost surreal.

"This is Karnataka, not Kerala," Adititeased.
"There are very nice massage places near the Virupaksha Temple. All the foreign tourists have put wonderful comments on Tripadvisor!" Meghna was her usual excited self.
"I hope you don't suggest that we go for it today?"
"Yes, actually I have just booked a slot for the two of us at 7.30!"
"You're just impossible, Meghna!" Aditi surrendered in frustration.

They called Maruti but he wasn't free, though he arranged for a replacement to come and pick them up from the hotel. It was already dark at 7:00 pm, when they started for the massage salon which was on the other side of town, opposite the temple compound; a twenty minutes' drive. The road was empty and pitch-dark, devoid of street lights; the only thing visible were the shadowy silhouettes of the old ruins in the distance.

The auto rickshaw halted with a rough jerk suddenly, in the middle of the road. Aditi clasped Meghna's arm inapprehension, her palm felt cold.
"I knew things won't go right. What will I tell Sandip if something happens to you?" she muttered under her breath.
"Just shut up! If something happens to me, you won't be in a position to give explanations either," Meghna snubbed her.
"What is it Bhaiya?" Meghna sounded confident while addressing the driver.
"I have run out of fuel Madam!" The driver seemed unperturbed.
"You ran out of fuel just like that?" Aditi exclaimed.
"So, what should we do now?" Meghna tried to take control, though by now she was nervous too.

"You take another auto, if one comes this way," the driver said, getting busy on his phone, speaking in Kannada, the local language. Within five minutes, a shadowy figure appeared on a motor bike; the man was well-built and knew the driver.
"Let's get down," Meghna whispered.
"But how can we escape on foot? This guy is on a bike!"
"I don't know, but it's safer to be in the open I feel. Just be quick," Meghna shoved Aditi.

They got down clumsily, but another auto rickshaw appeared from behind just at that moment. There was no way they could bypass this vehicle. Despite its blinding headlights, Meghna charged the driver as aggressively as she could.

"What is it? Why are you blocking our way?"

"I am here for you Madam!" It was unmistakably Maruti's voice; Meghna got a jolt.

"How did you know?"

"He called me saying he has run out of diesel. I called my boss to help him out and came myself to pick you up. That's my boss on the bike," he indicated towards that big built shadowy figure.

The ladies boarded the auto gratefully; Maruti appeared to be the real Sankat-Mochan (saviour) at this hour. His actions scaled a different height when he started his rickshaw and with his right foot kept pushing the other one; they moved like this for a while, till they reached a crossroad. The two ladies were in splits by now seeing his style of action, unmistakably influenced by the one and only Rajanikanth, the superstar.

"We will be late for our appointment, I hope they don't mind," Meghna remarked, now that they were on their way once again.

"I have already called them to postpone it for 15 minutes, don't worry," Maruti was unbeatable.

The salon was located in a long stretch of alley, dominated by old buildings converted into backpacker's hostels and trendy eateries. There were a few alleys in the area like this, bedecked with fancy roadside shops, interesting décor and colourful set ups; this place was dominated by budget travellers from Europe. The so-called salon was in a two-storey building. There was a restaurant on the ground floor; a narrow staircase took customers to the first floor, which was basically the residence of the owner. Two of the rooms in the dingy passageway were used as massage parlours it seemed.

"Is this what we get into after all the trouble?" Aditi was furious at her over-enthusiastic friend.
"It wasn't all that bad after all!" Meghna remarked after an hour on their way downstairs.
"It was surprisingly good and cheap too!" Aditi had to admit.

"Madam, if you are interested in watching the sunrise, we can go to Malvanta Hill at dawn tomorrow," Maruti suggested, as the auto rickshaw stopped at the hotel porch.
"Sunrise will be at what time?" Aditi enquired.
"Wait for me here at 5.30; that should be fine."
"Oh, yes, no problem, see you tomorrow!" Meghna intervened, leaving her friend exasperated.

***

"Let's have some Chinese food for dinner, we've earned it," Meghna suggested at dinner, she wasn't interested in the buffet it seemed. The dining room wasn't very crowded, only a pair of foreigners were enjoying some wine, post dinner.

"It looks like the others have already eaten their meal," Aditi made a casual remark.

"Madam, are you from Kolkata?" A young waiter arrived with the menu card. Aditi nodded, though a bit surprised at the question.

"I'm from Midnapore too, my name is Subhash Biswas," he smiled shyly.

"You've come so far from home for work?" Meghna expressed her surprise. On that the man explained that he and his friend from the same village had worked in this hotel for last three years; the money was good and they could send most of it home. As dinner progressed, Subhash brought his friend Bibek to their table; Meghna connected immediately with the two homesick men.

***

It was still dark when Maruti arrived the next morning. The slight nip in the air was a reminder of the missing winter. The foothills of Malvanta Hill were a ten-minute ride, located at the outskirt of the temple town. He parked the vehicle at the side of what seemed an illustrious temple, even in the hazy light of dawn.

"This is Raghunath Temple, we will come here on our return," Maruti explained.

The way to the top was a narrow rocky path, through the darkness of many caves; the single ray of Maruti's mobile torch was the only guiding light. It needed real fitness to manoeuvre this unknown terrain in semi darkness. Meghna kept chatting with Maruti, probably to ward off her nervousness. Aditi fell behind a bit, with her heavy backpack of camera equipment, though she was the more confident one. The prospect of a few brilliant sunrise shots was worth taking the risk, she had convinced herself.

That steep climb barefoot, on the narrow steps of the temple top, just to catch the Sunset at Bagan, she fondly remembered; it was their Myanmar trip a few months earlier. Meghna suffered from vertigo while coming down, while Aditi kept boosting her spirits from behind. They made it together and those sunset pictures were a treasure in her collection. Meghna, childlike at times, passionate and so full of life; she felt a tinge of affection for her friend.
She stumbled upon a stone while hurrying to catch up and lost her balance with her heavy load. A firm hand from behind prevented a fall.

"Hold my hand, it will be easier." In the thin light of the phone's torch, a compassionate face emerged like a dream.
"You're here?"
"I've also come for the sunrise," Bikram smiled. Their eyes locked together for what seemed like a very long moment before they resumed the climb. This time, Bikram held her hand in a firm grip till they reached the top. Meghna noticed this from a distance and purposely hurried Maruti ahead.

The hilltop was like a modest rocky terrace; there was a small group of European tourists, apart from Maruti's team. The eastern horizon was already displaying signs of a promising sunrise; it was a bunch of monkeys though that grabbed the attention of the foreigners.

"This is Kishkindhya, the ancient Kingdom of the Monkeys," Bikram explained, as Aditi appeared disconcerted at the sight of so many monkeys.
The magnificent sun overpowered the entire valley with a touch of molten gold in no time; everyone paused in awe.

"Maruti, do you know the meaning of your name?" Meghna whispered affectionately.
"Yes, Madam, Hanuman, the Lord of Kishkindhya." His face lit up with an enchanting smile.

On their way back, they entered the Raghunath Temple. Bikram also joined the team. It was believed that Lord, Rama along with his brother, Lakshman, took refuge here during the monsoon, before leading the final march towards Lanka. The beautiful relics and the ceremonial hall, with exquisite carvings of dancers, enthralled the sightseers.

"These carvings of couples and dancers suggest that this hall was primarily used for marriages in earlier times," Bikram stated.
"You are absolutely correct sir!" Maruti was impressed by Bikram's remark.
"What is your plan for rest of the day?"
"Maruti is suggesting Vittala Temple after breakfast. It will take half a day it seems," Meghna answered. By now, she was also on friendly terms with Bikram.
"We also plan to go there in the morning; hopefully Ma can take the strain."
"Is she seriously ill, or its just her age?" Aditi enquired.

"A bit of both; she has a heart condition."

"She looks quite formidable to me though," Aditi frowned at Meghna at this casual comment.

"She is, with her strength of character," Bikram smiled, he took it positively though.

***

The Vittala Temple was further away from Malavanta Hill, connected via the State Highway; about twenty minutes' drive from the hotel. It was a huge compound, on rocky terrain, by the River Tungabhadra. The road to the temple passed through the hills, with old ruins on both sides, a perfect set up, evocative of a glorious past. About two kilometres from the temple compound, there were low stone shelters on both sides. They had served as marketplaces and stables during the old times, Maruti informed. On the right side of the road was a beautiful stepped tank. It was a public bath for taking a dip to purify oneself before entering the temple, he also mentioned.

"This ancient marketplace, the bath, as if they are still in use, I can visualise you as a 15th century princess riding a chariot towards the temple," Meghna remarked dreamily.

"It's truly wonderful, very romantic," Aditi sighed.

"Yes, I can smell romance in the air!!" Meghna added; her intelligent eyes twinkling in humour.

The sprawling area of the temple compound was a visual treat to the tourists and the architecture was a photographer's delight. Aditi was taking an angled shot of the Grand Stone Chariot at the entrance when Ambika arrived with her entourage. She was supported by a walking stick and her doting son, Bikram. Shrirupa accompanied her, while Uma trailed behind with a supply of medicine and water; Nandni remained a few paces behind, probably to keep distance from the party to get some stolen moments of her own. Avijit was nowhere to be seen. Bikram and Aditi locked eyes from a long glance, signifying intimacy; Mrs. Ambika Deb didn't miss it.

The Vittala Temple was an architectural wonder in terms of grandeur and intricate carvings, undoubtedly the best tourist attraction in all of Hampi. There were many shrines and Mandapas (decorated halls) spread across the sprawling grounds, but the most notable ones were the Ranga Mandapa (entertainment hall), Kalyan Mandapa (marriage hall), Maha Mandapa (congregation hall), the main temple of Lord Vittala and the Devi shrine. One could distinguish the halls from the nature of carvings at their bases; the marriage hall depicted couples, the entertainment hall had sculptures of dancers, musicians and even had musical pillars that resonated like drums. The congregation hall was adorned with detailed carvings of war scenes.

Meghna was looking at the romantic sculptures at the base of the Kalyan Mandapa. She had chosen to explore on her own; Aditi was busy elsewhere. The figures looked so real in the soft glow of the morning sun. A royal wedding, a beautiful princess, a majestic king, chanting of Vedic hymns, it came so naturally in this set up, shemeditated. A restless voice from nearby interrupted her thoughts. She looked back at Nandini talking on her mobile phone in a corner, or rather trying to talk.

"Hello, Tiara! This is Mamma, can you hear me?" Her desperate attempt was futile though, the network was really poor at this remote location. Amid the serenity of the artistic backdrop, she cut astrange figure; agitated, helpless, as if a patch of darkness in the brilliant sky. Meghna quietly left thehall.

Ambika sat on the stairs of the main hall, it was clearly too difficult for her to cover the vast compound. She chose to visit only the main structure. Uma was by her side, giving her drinking water dutifully. Shrirupa too waited upon her for a while and then went out on her own; Bikram was looking at the structures, referring to a book on Hampi; she met him on her way out.

"You should have insisted that Avijit come along, it would have done him good," he remarked.

"I am tired of pushing him Dadabhai, he is not a kid!"

"I'm sorry, I didn't mean that. I thought you both would have enjoyed the day out together."

"He's better off alone, I need some time on my own too," she almost whispered. There was an awkward silence between them when Aditi arrived. She greeted Bikram; in turn he introduced her to Shrirupa; the atmosphere eased out.

"Hampi is the former capital of Vijaynagar and Vittala Temple is the jewel in its crown. This magnificent temple was built under the patronage of Devaraya II in the 15th century, but much of its present-day structures are attributed to the great ruler Krishna Devaraya." Bikram explained to Aditi at a later point, when they strolled away from the crowd to a small temple in the south-eastern corner.

"Hampi reminds me of Sharadindu babu's novel "By the Tungabhadra," Aditi remarked.

"What is it about?"

"It's about a princess falling in love with a commoner, defying the proposal of a mighty King; they met on a voyage on the Tungabhadra," she smiled enticingly.

"It sounds good in a fairy-tale; doesn't fit in the real world."

"You won't understand Bikram."

"Why won't I?"

"Because you are a wealthy businessman, there are things money can't buy."

"You are mistaken Madam; I belong to a wealthy business family, but I am nothing, not worth a penny." There was a sudden touch of sombreness in Bikram's voice that surprised Aditi.

"Sorry, don't know why I said this to you; we hardly know each other." Bikram was embarrassed by this sudden lapse.

"Bikram, we can be friends," her soft voice was compassionate. They remained silent for a long time, but the unspoken words resonated through the ancient walls of the temple arch.

***

"He is having toothache, that age old wisdom tooth problem of his," Meghna informed Aditi while talking to her husband Sandip over the phone. He was currently in Yangon for a conference.

"Let him have some Ibrufen, it should help; he has to carry on with work after all!" Aditi prescribed.

"No, Sandip, no painkiller! Yes, she suggested some, but I think you should manage without it. There is clove oil in the medicine pouch, apply that and also gargle with salted warm water." Meghna was stern with her instructions.

"This is absolute dictatorship, my heart goes out for the poor fellow," Aditi remarked, once Meghna finished her telephonic conversation.

"But, it's for his good only! At times I get confused whether you are my friend or his! Whose side would you take in case we fall out?"

"He is a gem, a perfect gentleman; if you two fall out, that would be your fault I have no doubt," Aditi was quick to respond.

"Wow! And all these years, I thought you are my friend!"

They decided to visit Virukaksha Temple and then explore the Hampi Bazar alleys, where they had gone for a massage earlier, once the sun lost some of its heat. They finished lunch on their return from

Vittala Temple and were now taking it easy in the hotel room.

"The Deb family is a bit complicated; don't you think?" Meghna remarkedidly.

"The family is not only complicated, but dysfunctional, if you ask me. That brother of Bikram's, I find him weird and the sister nervy; the mother is an absolute dictator, heavily controlling everyone's life," Aditi commented forcefully.

"Yes, I was overhearing the sister trying to make a call; she seems to have a daughter, who isn't accompanying her mother on holiday."

"Clearly, she is separated from her husband, the daughter must have gone to spend her holiday with the father and she is worked up about that. Bikram seems to be a lonely man too!" Aditi was thoughtful.

"You do like him!"

"Don't know, but he is very special, never felt like this before."

"I feel sorry for Dr. Arnab Bose!"

"What's there to feel sorry about? He's just a colleague."

"He is rather sweet on you, don't deny that!"

"He's a very career centric, selfish fellow, not my type at all."

"What about that CA guy, your sister's friend? You used to like him; I know."

"Who Soumen? He has a sweet girlfriend, we got introduced recently."

***

The Virupaksha Temple compound was a busy spot, with local devotees and a large number of tourists enjoying the beauty of the fine architecture. Meghna and Aditi went inside for Darshan of the deity, Virupaksha, a form of Lord Vishnu, after viewing the temple structure from the outside. It was dusk when they reached the Hampi Bazar alleys, the street shops were already illuminated, offering interesting merchandise, ranging from beads to anklets, garments, handcrafted bags and sandals. A shop offering sandalwood incense caught the attention of the ladies, who were both fond of fragrances. The shopkeeper was enthusiastic and his products seemed really good. They settled for a handful of items.

"Isn't that Bikram's brother?" Meghna remarked pointing towards a shaded corner, as Aditi was making the payment.

"Yes, that's Avijit, his brother; he seems to be alone!"

"Isn't it strange?"

"I told you, the entire family is strange. His wife looked very frustrated this morning," Aditi remarked pensively.

Afterwards, they went to a roadside restaurant, along with Maruti, for some coffee. The shop looked like a cheap copy of a European café from the décor, though the snacks they offered were really good.

"Who else is there in your family, Maruti?" Meghna was curious about the young man and had developed an affection for him; he was much younger and somehow reminded her of the brother she always longed for.

"I have my Amma and a younger brother, he goes to an English medium school," Maruti's face lit up with satisfaction. "My father passed away from excessive drinking when I was ten, I am twenty-three now. I had to drop out of school, so wanted my brother to study. He stays with me here, Amma is in the village."

"It must be hard for you to pay for his education!" Meghna was awestruck.

"Yes, but I manage. I work in a restaurant here during the late evenings, as a cook. The *phirang* (foreigner) customers like my cooking, they give me generous tips."

"Why don't you save some money and buy an auto rickshaw of your own? You can try for a bank loan even," Aditi suggested.

"Yes, I want to do that in future. Don't like my boss."

"No one likes their boss Maruti, you aren't an exception," Meghna joked.

"My boss is bad; he has two wives! One here and one in Goa," Maruti stuck to his point.

"But that makes him a bad husband, not a bad boss," Aditi's remark brought hearty laughter.

*** ***

Chapter 4

The Deb family had gathered in Ambika's room for afternoon tea, Uma was serving tea and snacks to everyone, while Nandini and Shrirupa showed their purchases to Ambika. They had gone for some post-lunch shopping to the nearby handloom shop. Ambika enjoyed such leisurely gatherings around her; it gave her a sense of emotional security. Nandini's mobile rang amidst the conversation and she hesitated momentarily before taking the call.

"Hello! It's me. Yes, I can talk." She sounded a bit nervous and went out of the room hurriedly.

"She seems to be too preoccupied with her phone lately," Ambika remarked, she was irritated by the interruption.

"Must be her kitty party friends," Shrirupa's voice reflected affection towards her sister-in-law.

"I don't think so; she's trying to stay in touch with Ankit."

"Tiara is with Ankit; they have gone to Corbett National Park with a few friends. Nandini talks to her," Shrirupa tried toreason.

"It wasn't Tiara on the phone; she calls from her own mobile. I have noticed it off late, the girl has so easily forgotten how they treated her," Ambika reproached. They continued with the ritual of tea, but the atmosphere had sobered.

"The tea has gotten cold. Was it Ankit on the phone?" Ambika confronted Nandini immediately on her return. Nandini muttered nervously, not knowing how to defend herself.

"I don't like it at all. He's trying to be on good terms just to get Tiara's custody. Don't be in any fancy illusion."

"Ma!" Nandini cried out, there were tears in her eyes.

"What's the harm if she wants to go back to Ankit? He never misbehaved with her." Bikram spoke out suddenly, taking Ambika by surprise.

"So, she already has some allies in the family? I guess I'm the last one to be informed, if any decision is taken!" Ambika sounded spiteful.

"Ma, don't you want all of us to be happy? She is old enough to decide for herself, let her do that!" Bikram tried to make peace, his voice soft with emotion.

"I know why you say this, I am old and sick, but I still notice everything." Ambika's knack for emotional blackmail worked. Bikram looked awkward.

"Damn this family drama!" Avijit, who was sitting in a corner stood up and left the room abruptly, which brought about an eerie silence.

***

The next morning, at the breakfast table, Ambika was reluctant to go for an outing.

"Nandini, Shri, if you are interested, we can go to the Virupaksha Temple, it isn't far from here, won't take long," Bikram suggested, in an attempt to cheer up the general mood, which was still sombre after last evening's episode. Everyone welcomed the idea, though Avijit chose to stay back once again.

"In that case, Uma can also come with us. I'm sure Avi can give company to Ma for an hour or two," Bikram suggested.

"It's not a vacation for her, she has come here as my attendant and my condition requires constant attention, you're probably forgetting that!" Ambika retorted in her usual authoritative way. Uma went pale at the hint of her status, Bikram looked embarrassed too.

"I want to apologise to you Uma," Bikram went to her before leaving for the temple.

"Please don't. You haven't done anything wrong. For that matter, Masi was right too. I have a duty and I am paid for it, my family needs this salary, which is quite generous for the market rate." She spoke in a matter-of-fact way, though Bikram cringed inwardly at her response.

***

"Will you go for a cruise on the Tungabhadra?" The WhatsApp message came when Aditi and Meghna were returning from their temple tour in the morning.

"Can you go to the Museum alone?" Aditi blushed, while suggesting.

"I can sense some adventure or is it a date?" Meghna joked, as she guessed the situation.

"Actually, we all can go together; Bikram is suggesting a cruise on the Tungabhadra."

"Come on, you know what they say – two's company but three's a crowd," Meghna laughed.

"I'm rather up for a ride to Maruti's village. You two have a good time," she further emphasised, affectionately.

***

In the mild afternoon breeze, Aditi and Bikram sailed on the blue waters of the Tungabhadra on a traditional Agarala boat, as if on an eternal voyage, with absolutely no human presence in the landscape. The Rocky Mountains, embedded with ancient cave temples on both banks and the glorious sky above remained witness to moments of intimacy, almost unreal.

"Tell me about the Princess in that novel," Bikram broke the silence.

"She was beautiful and bold," Aditi answered softly.

"Like you?"

"She was bold enough to turn down the king for the sake of love."

"Will you?"

"What?"

"Will you accept an ordinary man, someone who is nothing compared to you?" His voice was emotional.

"You aren't ordinary, Bikram," she looked up, her eyes were moist with suppressed emotion.

The setting sun painted the western sky in layers of crimson, a glow of molten gold caressed her lovely face. She rested her head on his shoulder with the shyness of a new bride.

***

"Ma, an employee in the fruit processing unit got hurt today. He has been admitted to the hospital. Two fingers on his right hand were badly crushed, otherwise he is stable. Khanna Uncle wants to discuss the compensation amount." Bikram had received a call from Mr. Khanna while returning from the cruise. He came to Ambika's room to give her the update. It was almost dinner time; she was resting on an armchair by the window, while Uma was making her bed, in preparation for bedtime.

"You should have put me on the call, instead of informing me now." Ambika sounded irritated. Uma left the room quickly, as the conversation was of a private nature.

"I was outside when he called; anyway, we need to decide on the amount among ourselves first."

"How did he manage to hurt himself? Our machines are safe, never had such an accident at the plant before!"

"Apparently this guy has drinking problems. He was warned several times by his supervisor."

"In that case, there's no question of compensation. He will drink it away anyway, even if we pay. We are taking care of the medical bills; we can give a job to one of his family members."

"His children are small, if we take his wife; the salary won't be the same, since she can't replace him."

"That's a price he has to pay for his vice, we can't create a bad precedence. In fact, I would like to issue a show cause notice to the supervisor; he should have sacked the man long ago."

"I don't agree with you in this matter; the family will suffer, not the man."

"You don't agree with me in a lot of matters nowadays, I can't help that."

"Ma!"

"Yes, I know the exact reason for your changed attitude." She was caustic.

"What are you hinting at?" Bikram was stern this time, losing his usual cool.

"It's that girl you're chasing; but let me tell you, she isn't our type, it won't work."

"Yes, she isn't your type, I agree, and probably won't fit in the family; but she is perfect for me and I care for her."

"So, you will defy your mother for that girl you hardly know?"

"I haven't said anything like that, nor thought of it. She may not find me worthy, though if she does, I shall go to any length to be with her. I didn't want to say these unpleasant words, you compelled me, Ma."

"Finally, you show your true colours. You've proved that you are not my son!" There was a momentary silence after she uttered those words.

"How could you say this Ma? You have been my mother; my world has revolved around you ever since my childhood." Bikram was dumbfounded, his voice choked.

"Your world was such a thin bubble that it burst at a single prod of an unknown girl." She mocked, completely ignoring his sentiment.

"You better send in Avijit. I'll discuss the matter of compensation with him and take the final decision. If Khanna Ji calls again, ask him to contact Avijit for this or any other official matter," she dismissed Bikram with finality. He took a few moments to let the words seep in and then left the room slowly.

***

The dining room wasn't crowded, a few guests sat here and there. Mrs Sethi and Sukhdev Saha were having dinner together, sitting by a window. It seemed that the simplicity of Saha had stricken a chord with the otherwise reticent Sunita; she enjoyed his company.

Bikram sat at a table alone. He looked devastated; there wasn't any food in front of him. He had come here without giving much thought to it, straight after the confrontation with Ambika. Sometime later, Shrirupa and Nandini also entered; Nandini was about to approach him, but looking at his expression decided otherwise. They settled at the next table instead. The ladies were chatting among themselves while waiting for Amibka to join them for dinner.

Ambika came in a few minutes later, accompanied by Uma, and straightway joined the ladies, without even sparing a glance at Bikram. They started with their dinner. It was clear that Avijit wasn't joining them; Shrirupa placed some food and a glass of water at Bikram's table silently. Uma brought Ambika's food from the buffet, everyone started eating, and the mood remained sombre at their table. Bikram didn't touch his food, there was a faraway look in his eyes; his handsome face looked vulnerable with some internal emotional turmoil.

While Uma was fetching water for Ambika, she got a bowl of custard for Bikram; she kept it in front of him gently.

"You like custard," she smiled and then departed with the water.

Ambika started hiccupping while eating. She, Uma and Shirupa reached out for her glass of water at the same time. The water spilled in the commotion and the glass fell to the ground, breaking intopieces. Bikram offered his own glass, which he hadn't touched. The hiccups subsided with the water and Ambika resumed eating, though she still didn't acknowledge Bikram's presence.

"Leave the Rajma, Ma; have kheer instead," Shrirupa offered. Ambika accepted it. Kheer was her favourite dessert, and the hotel buffet had a wide variety, she thought gratefully. Nandini eagerly offered a roti to her mother from her own plate. Ambika smiled affectionately; it was apparent that they both wanted to get over the bitterness of the previous evening.

"Are you feeling hot, Ma?" Nandini remarked in a while, noticing her mother perspiring profusely.

"The AC isn't working properly it seems, aren't you feeling hot too?" Ambika sounded agitated.

"After you finish your meal, I'll check your blood pressure, just to be cautious," Uma intervened. That was when Ambika collapsed on her chair. Bikram sprinted up to provide support, Nandini cried out for help. The hotel supervisor rushed to their aid and Ambika was rushed off to the local hospital quickly.

"It's the food that made her sick!" Nandini said accusingly, out of nervousness, though Shrirupa scolded her for that, as they were leaving for hospital. The floor manager was present at that moment and he didn't take the allegation kindly.

"We take utmost care to maintain hygiene, this isn't fair Madam. Anyway, just for your assurance, we will get all the food on your table tested." He was angry and embarrassed, as the complaint came in front of other customers dining at that time.

Ambika was taken to the ICU, where she breathed her last within half an hour. The hospital authorities

informed the police, since the attending doctors
sensed some foul play.

***   ***

64

Chapter 5

Sub Inspector Sridhar came to the hotel in the middle of the night; he came with his team from the nearby Hampi tourism police station. Based on the tip off by the hospital, he started the basic enquiry; also collected the food samples and sealed Ambika's room, after talking to the hotel manager. his superior would join the investigation once the autopsy report was ready, Sridhar informed.

"I want to go to the hospital, Meghna!" Aditi urged, when she learned about the death.

"You can't just barge in Aditi; he may feel awkward in front of his family. Talk to him once he comes back," Meghna tried to reason, while calming her frienddown. They remained awake all night, wrought with tension.

The Deb family came back from the hospital in the wee hours of the next morning after finishing all the formalities.

"I am really sorry for your loss, it's unthinkable!" Aditi approached the family after breakfast, they were gathered in Avijit's room; Bikram was missing from the group.

"Where is Bikram?" Aditi asked Shrirupa, after a moment's hesitation.

"He has locked himself in his room, refusing to come out. Maybe you can talk some sense into him," Aditi blushed at the suggestion, but took her leave at that.

***

Aditi knocked on the door softly a few times; initially there wasn't any response and then came an agitated cry, "Leave me alone, I beg you all!"

"It's me, Bikram," her voice had a soothing effect. There was silence from the other side of the door, but she waited patiently; the door opened in a while. She felt a tinge of pang seeing the distressed figure standing in front of her. Without waiting for hisinvitation, she went inside; Bikram didn't protest, he silently closed the door behind her. The atmosphere of the room reflected grief, with the drawn curtains, unlit lamps and that shadowy frame of Bikram.

"I know it's a great loss for you, but you must hold yourself together as the head of the family now. Mrs. Deb would have wanted it." She touched his shoulder. He completely broke down at her assuring presence.

"I am to blame for all this!"

"Don't blame yourself for something that was beyond your control!"

"You don't know anything, Aditi; you don't know what happened between us. I was a disgrace! She is gone with a lot of pain and now I will have to live with the regret for the rest of my life." Aditi didn't know how to respond, since she was unaware of the facts.

***

SI Sridhar handed the autopsy report to Mr. M. Kannan, Superintendent of Police. It had been two days since the death had occurred.

"Interesting!" Kannan remarked, looking at it. SP Kannan was a young IPS officer in his mid-thirties. His closely cropped hair and thick moustache gave him a tough look, though it couldn't disguise his handsomeness. His intelligent eyes were expressive and carried a touch of humour, whenever he was in a light mood. His service record so far had been impeccable.

"Do you think it was an overdose, Sir?"

"If we go by the report, yes." Kannan referred to the autopsy report that mentioned the presence of cocaine in large quantities in the victim's stomach.

"That means the lady was an addict!" Sridhar expressed surprise.

"It can also mean that someone else mixed it in her food." There was subtle sarcasm in his tone. Kannan proceeded to Hotel Ambassador after that, he had officially started his investigation.

***

"It's ridiculous to accuse the management of serving adulterated food; no one else fell ill eating that meal!" The hotel manager sounded agitated when Kannan met him.

"We haven't said any such thing, have we? Of course, if any of your staff purposely tampered with her food, that's different." The manager went pale at that, though kept up his defensive stance.

"Why should they do such a thing? Most of them come from outside the state, they are focused in earning their living."

"Who knows why? Let me meet all the staff members who were on duty in the dining hall that evening."

The interrogation began; each staff member was encouraged to describe the sequence of events individually, to cross-check the details.

"So, the lady was having kheer when she collapsed and it was given to her by her daughter-in-law?" Kannan picked up the trail, as one of the staff members attending Mrs. Sethi at a nearby table mentioned the incident.

"I think she was having it with a roti that her own daughter offered," the waiter added nervously.

"So, the plot thickens!" Kannan muttered under his breath.

***

Kannan started questioning the Deb family after finishing his initial enquiry. The hotel manager had set up an office for the investigative team in a small banquet hall on the ground floor. All the members of the family were called to this office one by one, to be questioned in private.

"You were present at the crime scene; could you describe the sequence of events to me?" Kannan was blunt in his approach; Bikram was the first one to be interviewed.

"Crime scene? Has it been established that it was a crime?" Bikram reacted to the question.

"Do you think I would have wasted my time here, if it wasn't one?"

"I wasn't paying much attention to the surroundings. I only became alert when she collapsed."

"Any particular reason for such oblivion?"

"I was worrying about a recent accident that occurred at the factory."

"The accident bothered you so much that you didn't even touch your food?"

"What do you mean?"

"Mrs. Deb was your stepmother, I gather?"

"She was my mother and always will remain so," Bikram said emphatically; he was running out of patience fast.

"Were you a son to her too or merely a stepson? By the way, I will require the contact details of your family lawyer." Kannan nudged him before changing the subject. He decided not to question Bikram further now and called for Avijit instead.

Avijit arrived with a grumpy face; he was quiet and answered mostly in monosyllables. His behaviour wasn't related to the recent loss, Kannan picked that up immediately. The officer observed him more closely and his eyes lit up with a sudden understanding.

"What do you do for living, Mr. Deb?"

"We have a business in Rudrapur."

"A family business; but what's your role in it exactly?" Avijit looked uncomfortable and then answered weakly.

"I am starting a real estate business, a diversification."

"Where were you during the time of the mishap, that is on Wednesday evening between 7.30 and 8.30 pm?"

"I was in my room and then went for a walk."

"Why didn't you go for dinner?"

"I wasn't hungry."

"You were alone in your room?"

"Yes, I went for a walk down the road, after my wife left for dinner."

"How long have you been married?"

"It's been three years."

"You can go for now and please send your wife in."

Shrirupa entered the interrogation room with an air of confidence and poise, the opposite of her husband. Kannan was impressed. He asked her to describe the sequence of events and she did so in minute detail, which corroborated the accounts of the hotel staff.

"You are from Kolkata; do you like a small town like Rupdrapur?" This question unsettled her for the first time, though she recovered quickly enough and agreed smilingly.

"What do you do, Madam?"

"I am a homemaker."

"What did you do before marriage?"

"I was a high school teacher of Mathematics."

"You don't miss that career?"

"A married woman needs to prioritise." The conversation ended with that. It was Nandini's turn next.

Nandini was nervous from the beginning, though she described the dinner sequence quite accurately.

"You know, the hiccups almost choked her; she always liked Rajma Chawal, but it didn't suit her that day. She was enjoying her meal afterwards, everything looked so normal and then suddenly this happened." She broke down. Kannan gave her some time, before questioning her further.

"You are still quite young, haven't you considered remarriage, Madam?" Nandini wasn't prepared for the question and was visibly surprised.

"We aren't officially divorced yet." She almost whispered.

"Do you do anything for a living?"

"Not as such. Ma thought I should take it easy after all that stress."

"Are you close to your sister-in-law?"

"Yes, she's like an older sister to me; I look up to her in many ways."

"So, you two were generally together through all your days here?"

"Yes, but why?"

"Has your brother always been this quiet? How is his relationship with his wife?"

"He's an introvert, but not a bad person, you know! He withdraws under pressure." Nandini became defensive instantly.

"Who puts pressure on him, his wife or his mother?" She was offended at the question and refused to answer. Kannan allowed her to leave at this point.

Uma was calm, with a certain professionalism that explained her position in the household; but a shadow of grief was unmistakable in her eyes. She described the incident well, even hinted that she felt the hiccup probably was an early sign of a heart attack. Kannan ignored her remark and refused to reveal any information on the cause of death.

"How long have you been with the family?"

"About a year."

"Did the Debs appoint you through an agency?"

"Not really; I am related to the family. Mrs. Ambika Deb was a cousin of my mother."

"Whcrc did you work before this?"

"I was with a nursing home for three years, after finishing my training. But they weren't confirming me, so I left that job and started freelancing for patients through an agency in Delhi. It was Mehta Associates. I'll will give you their contact details. Last year, Masi fell ill; she was admitted in a Delhi hospital. Ma and I went to see her and then I accompanied her to Rudrapur after she was discharged from the hospital."

"So, you knew all the family members before?"

"I knew Avijit da, went to meet him two-three times while he was studying in Delhi; Bikram da came home once, during a visit to Avijit da. I met Boudi and Nandini later."

"How is it so? Hadn't you been to Rudrapur before?"

"No, we weren't really that close; my mother contacted Masi after Dad passed away in an accident. She helped us from time to time."

"Was it more out of gratitude that you went to Rudrapur?"

"The money was good and yes; Ma felt a bit obligated too."

***

After finishing the initial round of interviews with the Deb family, Kannan called for Mrs. Sethi and Sukhdev Saha. They were the ones among the Indian tourists at the hotel who were present in the dining hall at the time of the incident.

Mrs. Sethi appeared confident, though a bit displeased at being dragged into such an incident, especially during her vacation. She maintained her poise and described the crime scene sincerely.

"The elder boy came first, he looked very disturbed; then came the two girls of the family. The lady came a bit later, accompanied by the attendant. There was a lot of tension among them, we could sense that even from a distance. Then she started hiccupping quite violently; the commotion started from there actually. Everyone tried to help at the same time and ended up breaking the glass of water. Finally, the boy gave her some water. Then I wasn't paying much attention to that table until she collapsedabruptly."

"Could you tell us about the family, since you've seen them for the past few days?"

"The lady was quite an authoritarian, the younger boy and his sister meek; the elder boy looked decent and the daughter-in-law quite sensible. Beyond this, it's difficult for me to judge."

"Do you think it is possible for anyone to hold a grudge against the deceased?"

"You mean to say a grudge strong enough to kill her?" Mrs. Sethi reacted sharply; Kannan nodded.

"I don't know, but she was quite arrogant; it's possible she antagonised quite a few people over the course of her life, but whether she managed to provoke someone at the hotel, I can't tell."

"Madam, please don't leave the hotel without informing us," Kannan made a parting remark.

Sukhdev Saha was eager to help the police with his statement, he even offered to extend his stay in Hampi, if needed. Kannan acknowledged his sincerity and started the interrogation.

"Do you think there was some tension in the family, especially during that dinner?"

"The lady was insecure and wanted to be the centre of attention all the time; it happens when a fierce personality falls sick and starts losing their hold over things. It's always hard on the younger generation, you know. I have seen my grandfather like that. Even while he was bedridden, he would try to control every decision in the family. My father and uncles suffered. Towards the end, even they secretly started counting his last days," Saha sighed, lost in his own thoughts.

"Her son was hurt, it showed on his face and she was enjoying it. It was apparent; she was being cruel," He added after a pause.

"Do you know the reason for it?"

"It's that girl; the lady didn't approve of her from the very beginning. Intelligent, sensible, independent; I wish my son falls for someone like her."

"Please elaborate Mr. Saha," Kannan was interested to dig into this new angle.

'That girl from Kolkata - Aditi, I think, I'm talking about her. The elder son is smitten by her charm; it is quite obvious. I feel that created some friction between mother and son."

"Do you think this could lead even to murder?" Kannan was abrupt. Saha was taken aback at first and then gave it some thought.

"Couldn't say. It isn't normal for a son to kill his mother."

"He is a stepson." Saha looked surprised.

"I didn't know..." The interrogation ended at that.

***

Bikram was avoiding Aditi ever since the police started their investigation and she was deeply hurt by it.

"It's natural, Aditi. He isn't ready for you yet, give him some time," Meghna tried to reason.

"Why should he do this to me?"

"He is suffering from a guilty conscience, I believe."

"But why?" Aditi was exasperated.

"Who knows what happened within the family! Don't judge him." Meghna held her friend's hand inempathy.

It was almost afternoon, Aditi and Meghna were having a late lunch. At that point, SP Kannan sent for them.

He started with Aditi; his manner was friendly, with an undertone of professionalism.

"You are a doctor, so you must have good knowledge of the vulnerabilities of heart patients, I assume?"

"I work in the cardiology department," Aditi replied in a flat tone.

"I see. Mrs. Deb died of a cardiac arrest." He made a statement.

"Patients with a weak heart always run that risk," she remarked.

"It can be engineered at times too, isn't it?"

"What do you mean?"

"Nothing as such. By the way, you and Bikram are good friends I hear. Do you have any idea why he was so upset last Wednesday during dinner?"

"I didn't even know that he was upset."

"Where were you that evening between 7.30 to 8.30 pm?"

"Meghna and I went out for dinner near the Virupaksha Temple area. By the time we came back Mrs. Deb had already been taken to the hospital."

It was Meghna's turn to be questioned next; although it was she, who started with a question for the SP.

"You suspect murder, don't you?"

"Why do you think so? It could be an accident or a suicide too."

"The Superintendent of Police won't come for an investigation merely for a suicide, Sir," she smiled charmingly. He observed her closely, a tinge of humour appeared in his eyes.

"What do you do, Madam?"

"I am a lecturer; you already know that I'm sure."

"What else do you do?" he smiled.

"I'm a writer; I write mystery novels."

"I anticipated something along those lines. Hope you don't find police officers stupid!"

"Absolutely not, but lazy at times; in my book, Sir!" The conversation turned to the actual interrogation after that.

"How would you describe the Deb family?"

"Dysfunctional."

"What do you mean?"

"None of them were happy or normal, I felt. The couple are mismatched, and the wife dissatisfied with her husband. The daughter is nervy and desperate for love. Mrs. Deb was a tyrant; pardon my words for the departed soul."

"What about Bikram?"

"He's a gentleman, but a bit soft in his nature, probably under constant pressure from his mother."

"Do you think any of them could have plotted a murder?"

"So, the family is under scanner?" Meghna became alert suddenly.

"It's just a possibility."

"That's difficult for me to say, I hardly know them. Killing one's own mother isn't easy."

"What if it's a stepmother or mother-in-law?"

"Are you suspecting Bikram, Sir?" She paled at the suggestion.

"I'm suspecting everyone at this moment, Madam, the hotel staff, even your friend," he gave a sardonic smile.

"Are they in love, Bikram and Aditi?" he continued.

"Love is a very deep word; they like each other, I know only that much."

"Please don't leave the hotel without informing us," he cautioned customarily, before ending the conversation.

"Trust me, Sir, we won't... before seeing the end," she gave a smile before leaving the room.

***

"The situation isn't looking good for Bikram at this moment," Meghna remarked, as she and Aditi went for a stroll.

"Do you think they suspect him of some foul play? It was a cardiac arrest, the SP told mehimself." Aditi was nervous.

"Come on, we all know it's murder they're investigating; only we don't know the cause of death. Some kind of poison is my guess."

"How can Bikram poison her, he wasn't even seated with her. If it is a murder, it has to be one of the hotel staff."

"It's comforting probably to put the blame on outsiders, but even then, someone may have used the staff to do it. What motive could an outsider have?"

"What motive did Bikram have?"

"Plenty; in the eyes of the police of course. For that matter, each one of the family had a motive; the common one being financial independence."

"You are ruthless, Meghna!" Aditi was hurt.

"I'm being practical; there isn't anything personal and you know that. I suggest you try to think rationally too, don't get too emotional about it; keep some distance with Bikram for the time being."

"He has distanced himself from me already, I don't why."

"He is behaving responsibly, I would say. He cares for you Aditi, that's why he doesn't want you to be dragged into this mess."

"Do you think the police will implicate him?" Aditi tried to hold back tears.

"Not unless they get some evidence against him. One thing is bothering me though, you know; why did Mrs. Deb hiccup so violently? It must have some connection with the murder."

"Do you think the rajma was poisoned?"

"Maybe so, or maybe she took something just before dinner that caused the poisoning."

"It's all so confusing, I wish we hadn't come for this vacation." Aditi was frustrated.

***

The next few days were quite eventful. SP Kannan got search warrants and initiated a search operation through the rooms of every member of the Deb family. He even searched the staff quarters. Some cocaine was seized from a little pillbox-like container in Avijit's room. It had two layers, the top one stored cigarette, but the lower one contained some cocaine in a pouch. The quantity wasn't much, though enough for an addict. Avijit initially denied any knowledge of the pouch, but when Kannan insisted on a blood test, he finally succumbed and admitted to being an addict. Avijit was booked for having an illegal substance in his possession. The family lawyer, who had already arrived, arranged for a bail in 24 hours' time.

SP Kannan started questioning the family once again, since the situation demanded that he look into the possibility of the family members having access to that cocaine.

"Did you know that your husband takes cocaine?" Shrirupa was the first one he started interrogating this time.

"Yes, I did."

"How long have you known about it?"

"I came to know about it right after our marriage." There was bitterness in her voice.

"Didn't his mother put him in rehab or something to get rid of the addiction?"

"She got him married instead; I'm supposed to be his counsellor cum nanny or whatever you want to call it."

"Do you feel betrayed, Madam, by this marriage?"

"Not only me, but my parents were deceived too; they are heartbroken about it," she vented.

"Who else knows about this in the family?"

"Everyone."

"Do they also know where he keeps his supply?"

"He hasn't been discrete about it; so, it's easy to know. Dadabhai even threw out his supply a number of times in the past, in order to control him."

"I want you to remember the people who came to your room since the morning last Wednesday. Please don't leave out the hotel staff."

"Do you think it was taken from his supply on that day itself?"

"If it was taken earlier, your husband would have noticed it and talked about it to you, don't you think?" Kannan was observing Shrirupa's expressions minutely. She was thoughtful, trying to concentrate.

"In the morning, when we went for breakfast, Nandini came to call me. She waited inside the room as I was getting ready in and out of the bathroom. Avijit had already left by then, probably to have a smoke. After breakfast we went out to visit Virupaksha Temple; Ma, Uma and Avijit stayed back. After returning from there, I rested a while in my room, Avijit was also there. Housekeeping had already cleaned up during my absence in the morning. I don't know whether Avijit was in the room at that time. In the afternoon, Nandini and I had tea together in her room; Uma came to me to ask for some digestive tablets, her stock had run out. She said Avijit wasn't opening the door; he has this habit of spending hours in the bathroom. I gave her the room card, which she returned to me after she had helped herself to the tablets. She knows where I keep my medicine pouch. I stayed in Nandini's room till dinner time and then we left together for the dining room."

"Where did Avijit keep his cigarette case in the hotel room?"

"It was on the dressing table, along with my toiletries."

"One more question, Madam; haven't you thought of a divorce?" She took some time before answering.

"It's not an easy decision for a woman from a middle-class family, especially when the opponent is Mrs. Ambika Deb." Shrirupa took her leave after that.

Kannan called for Avijit next; this time he was submissive in his attitude and ready to cooperate in any way. He narrated his routine for last Wednesday, as was asked.

"I went to the staircase for a smoke before breakfast, as Shri was getting ready. Then after breakfast, I was in my room until the housekeeping staff came knocking. I left the room and spent some time in the garden and then chatted a while with Ma, before going back to my room. In the evening I went out for a stroll as I mentioned earlier, I didn't want dinner."

"You spent quite some time in the bathroom in the afternoon, did you hear anyone coming into your room that time?"

"I wasn't really concentrating you know! But yes, Dada came once, he realised I am in the bathroom, so he talked to me through the door and then left."

"What did he tell you?"

"He said that Ma wanted me to go to her room."

"How did he get in?" Avijit pondered over the question, he clearly hadn't thought of it earlier.

"I don't know, Shri may have opened the door for him. When I came out Shri wasn't around though."

"When did you realise that your cocaine stock had depleted by a large quantity?"

"Not on that day, it was much later, the next day actually." He faltered while answering.

"That means, on Wednesday evening, you had already used your quota and didn't need anymore, is that so?" Avijit didn't answer.

"Did you tell your wife or anyone else about the missing stock?"

"No, I didn't; I was scared." Avijit almost whispered.

"What were your scared of? Did you anticipate it was a case of cocaine poisoning?"

"When the police came the next morning to investigate and then later in the day, I realised most of my stock is gone, I sensed a connection between the two incidents."

"Aren't you close enough to your wife to discuss such serious matters?"

"We have our share of disagreements, especially in relation to my habits."

"What are the other topics of disagreements, may I ask?"

"She wanted to relocate to Kolkata, take up a teaching job; she also wanted me to find a job."

"So, you didn't want all these things?"

"It was out of the question; Ma wouldn't have agreed. Moreover, we are comfortable in our family home. I can start my own business; why should I work for someone else?"

"I see. You may go now."

It was Bikram's turn the next.

"I want to know in detail about what you did on last Wednesday, from the morning till dinner time."

"We had breakfast and then I took Shri and Nandini to Virupaksha Temple. I was in my own room for some time after that and then went out for sightseeing in the afternoon."

"Did you go out with someone?"

"I was with Aditi; we went to see the Tungabhadra River," he hesitated before replying.

"After that, what did you do?"

"I got an urgent call from the office while on our way back. So, I went to Ma's room to talk about it. After the discussion I went for dinner."

"From her room you went straight to the dining room?"

"Yes, I was hungry."

"Not hungry enough to eat I suppose? You didn't eat anything at dinner that day."

"I told you I was upset."

"Upset from an argument with your mother?"

"That's not true!"

"Your heated argument was quite audible from the outside, we have witnesses." Bikram looked uncomfortable at the remark, though he tried to recover quickly.

"Yes, we had a disagreement regarding the terms of compensation for the injured employee and it turned a bit personal. She asked me to send Avi in at the end, so I went to his room, conveyed the message and then headed for the dining room.”

“How did you enter Avijit’s room? He was in the toilet at that time, I know that.”

“Yes, Shri wasn’t around, but Uma was there, she let me in and told that Avijit was in the toilet and then she left. I hardly waited for a minute, told him to meet Ma and then left the room, closing the door behind me.”

“Did you know where he kept his cocaine stock?”

“I didn’t know exactly, but it isn’t hard to find out; he has a pattern of keeping his personal stuff.”

“Thank you for being honest with us,” the meeting ended with cordiality from Kannan’s side.

“I was with Masi all through that day, except the time when Bikram da and Masi were having a discussion in the evening. I ran out of digestive tablets; Masi needed them often. I knew Boudi kept a stock, so I went to her room. It was locked and no one answered. Then I thought of checking Nandini’s room, they are often together. There, I found Boudi, she gave me the room card. I went inside, took the medicine and was about to come out when Bikram da also came there.” Uma was narrating her movements on the fateful Wednesday.

“Was Avijit inside at that time?”

“Yes, I heard some noise from the washroom; he has a habit of sitting in the toilet for long hours.”

"Did you see Bikram leaving?"

"No, I didn't wait for that; Masi would have needed me, so I rushed back."

"Do you think Bikram had a fight with his Mother?"

"I don't know, I wasn't there, as I told you." She was careful.

"Was Mrs. Deb disgruntled with her elder son for some reason? You were her day and night companion after all, you should have some idea."

"I was a paid companion, Sir; there's a difference. The rich have their own share of complications, unlike us with simple problems of basic needs."

***

"Was cocaine the cause of death?" Meghna approached Kannan in his makeshift office at the hotel. They had by now established a good rapport, though not entirely informal.

"Yes, that's what the autopsy said. Getting the source was important; Avijit showed all the signs of an addict."

"Now that I think of it; one day Aditi and I spotted him in the hippie alleys behind Virupaksha Temple. He was alone, not on a touristic visit; that was apparent. Do you think it's his wife who actually committed the crime?"

"I can't say anything without proof, Madam, but that could be a strong possibility. She had enough reason of her own to do it."

"The rajma and the hiccups, I have an eery feeling about that, Sir; somehow I feel it has a strong connection with the murder."

"We need the chemical analysis report to zero down on that. In the meantime, if you can get some inside information, that will be helpful." Kannan smiled.

***

Aditi and Meghna went for a day trip to Badami Caves; Maruti's boss provided for the car and Kannan didn't object to the outing. It was a three and half hours' drive from Hampi. They started early to reach at the opening hour. The 6th century cave temples were located on the Badami Hills, at four different levels. A UNESCO heritage site, the caves were numbered from one to four. One needed to trek up the steps on foot to reach them. A fifth cave had been discovered recently, which was out of bounds for tourists at the moment.

The first temple was mainly dedicated to Lord Shiva, with intricate carvings of Nataraja and the other forms of the God. The second temple depicted both Lord Shiva and Lord Vishnu, along with other Gods. The sculpture of Harihara and Ardhanarishwara being the most prominent among them. The third and largest cave was dedicated to Lord Vishnu; its intricate carvings were a photographer's delight. The fourth cave was a Jain temple, dedicated to Lord Tirthankara.

It took quite some effort to reach the third cave for Meghna and Aditi, given that it was a steep hike. Meghna was out of breath and wanted to rest. The brilliant blue of the adjacent Agastha Lake came into view from the gap between two rocks, as they approached a platform. It was mesmerising, contrasted against the white clouds and bright sky above. The Bhootnath Temple at its bank, with its marvellous architecture, was picture-perfect, a reminder of the gloriouspast. No one was around to make noise. The morning breeze brushed against their face soothingly, as the duo spent time soaking in the site, silence prevailed except for cuckoo calls.

Aditi was busy in taking photographs of the beautiful sculptures inside the cave; Meghna sat on the veranda wondering about the zenith India had once reached, in science and architecture. At a time in the 6Th century, when the area around must have been a dense forest, in her romantic mind, she imagined an artisan working alone in this cave, sculpting an amorous Yaksha couple. A flower-girl came to visit him every day here, took care of his daily needs; could the face of Yakshini be that of the girl the artisan was very much in love with? She dreamily felt a connection with that sculpture, "Was I the flower-girl in some previous birth? Who knows!" She wanted to write a poem for Sandip, her husband; she suddenly missed him very much.

***

After a long yet satisfying day, Aditi and Meghna sat for dinner at the hotel's dining hall. It was time for a cosy drink and sumptuous food. Bibek came to their table to take the order. They exchanged pleasantries; the police had searched his and

Subhash's rooms, he mentioned, since they both were on duty during dinner that fateful evening.

"Did you witness everything that night?" Meghna asked him.

"Yes, more or less; I was at the buffet counter."

"Did you notice anything unusual?"

"Unusual? No! But the lady was probably not well, she looked very sombre that day from the beginning."

"What was so unusual about that?" Aditi made a caustic remark.

"Bikram Sir looked very sad too; Shrirupa Madam took some food and water for him; he didn't touch any of it."

"Can you remember who brought rajma to Mrs. Deb?" Meghna diverted the topic.

"Oh, yes, it was her attendant. She took some food and rice from the counter; rajma was among them."

"Now tell me, is it possible that the rajma was poisoned? Maybe by the attendant or someone from her table?" Bibek took some time at that, before adding his own views.

"I don't know if it was done at her table, but here I was manning the counters along with two other staff members. Why are you questing about the rajma, Madam? Is it because of the hiccups? The lady used to eat very unhealthy for her age, all rich food and very spicy at that, she ate a lot of chillies too."

"I still feel the hiccups were an early sign of a heart attack and Bibek is right, food like rajma is too rich for a heart patient," Aditi remarked. They dropped the topic at that and started discussing their Badami trip; Bibek left their table, after taking the order for dinner.

***

It was another Wednesday, the hotel lounge was busy with its usual business, a few new guests had arrived that morning, mostly foreigners, but Mr. Khanna was also among them. He had come to provide support to the family; they had arranged for Ambika's last rites to be held that day; a four-day ritual, since it was an unnatural death.

Meghna and Aditi went to the Museum across the road after lunch. While returning to the lounge, Aditi spotted Bikram sitting alone in the garden, lost in thought. He hadn't shaved his head, as the ritual demanded for sons, she noticed.

"Why are you sitting here alone?" As she approached Bikram, Meghna withdrew discretely.

"We just came back from the temple; the others have gone back to their rooms."

"You didn't shave off your head!"

"Oh, I didn't need to; I am not a bloodline to her, the priest pronounced. Avijit performed the ceremony, I merely offered my prayers." There was deep emotion in his voice.

"Let's have some tea. Have you eaten anything?" Aditi wanted to comfort him in her own way.

They were having tea together when a hotel employee came to give a message from the SP.

"He has requested your presence at his office here, Sir."

"Why is he summoning you of all people?" Aditi exclaimed, after the waiter left, she was disturbed.

"Maybe for some further enquiry; I'd better go and check." Bikram stood up.

"I'm coming with you." Aditi followed himresolutely, she called Meghna on her mobile on the way.

SP Kannan was questioning Mrs. Sethi in his office, a file remained open on his desk.

"As per you earlier statement, it was Bikram who offered her the water; do you still agree with that?"

"Yes, I saw him doing so, since her own glass broke due to the commotion."

Shrirupa and Nandini were waiting outside the office, they were relieved to see Bikram; Shrirupa was called inside as Mrs. Sethi left, Meghna arrived there at that moment. She quickly summed up the situation and joined the departing Mrs. Sethi for a private chat.

"What happened when your mother-in-law started having the hiccups? Could you please repeat the scene once again?" Kannan asked Shrirupa, she was surprised, yet answered confidently.

"We all reached out for the water at the same and because of that, the glass broke. Then Dadabhai offered his own glass of water. The hiccups subsided in a while."

"That's all for now, please send Ms. Nandini in."

Nandini was asked the same question and her answer matched Shrirupa's. Bikram was called in next. By then Meghna had returned after her brief chat, she and Aditi followed him inside.

"Mr. Bikram Deb, I am going to take you under custody on the charge of murdering Mrs. Ambika Deb. You can choose not to answer any of my questions from now onwards and also appoint a lawyer," Kannan declared professionally.

"What proof do you have against him?" Aditi shouted.

"I am not answerable to you, Madam, please leave unless you are his lawyer," Kannan responded sternly. Meghna tried to restrain her friend and suggested she inform the family of the arrest.

"What did you find against me officer, do I get to know that?" Bikram asked calmly.

"It's the chemical analysis report I guess?" Meghna remarked.

"Yes, none of the food contained any harmful substance, but one of the three glasses on the table contained high levels of cocaine in its residue. It's called circumstantial evidence, Madam Doctor." Kannan targeted Aditi in his end remark.

*** ***

Chapter 6

It was almost midnight, Aditi sat by the window looking out at the moonlit night; her face silhouetted like some classic painting in that soft glow. The sleeping figure of Meghna and the rhythm of her soft breathing suggesting a sense of tranquility, quite opposed to the turn of events of that day.

"Are you still awake?" Meghna remarked sleepily after a while, probably disturbed by the glow from the window.

"How are they treating him in the lock up?"

"Don't trouble yourself with such thoughts Aditi, it won't help the situation." Meghna was fully awake by now.

"I still can't believe he will be convicted for murder!"

"He won't, if he isn't guilty."

"If! Do you have any doubt about his innocence?"

"I have doubts about the entire findings; something isn't sitting right with it. But now you should rest Aditi; you won't be of any help to him if you become an emotional wreck." Meghna forced her friend to draw the curtain and go to her bed.

"Tomorrow is another day with new sunshine; night dear!" Her own voice reflected a touch of emotion this time.

***

"What's your lawyer doing Shrirupa, isn't he trying for Bikram's bail?" Shrirupa was having breakfast, sitting at a corner in the garden alone. Aditi had approached her on the way to the dining hall; Meghna wanted to stop her friend, but followed her instead, noticing herresolve.

"He will try his best of course, but looking at the evidence, he isn't very hopeful at the moment." Shrirupa was surprised at the sudden aggression from someone she hardly knew; yet answered calmly.

"What do you mean not hopeful? He managed to get bail for your husband so promptly and now it's difficult?" Aditi blurted out.

"Aditi, it's a case of murder. So far, the evidence is against him," Meghna tried to reason, she was embarrassed of her friend's outburst. Shrirupa wasempathetic, she didn't take offence.

"Didi, our situation is equally punishing. We aren't in a position to face anyone here; we feel ashamed to go to the dining room, everyone stares at us weirdly."

"She's really upset you know; it seems so unfair!" Meghna tried to explain.

"Don't you think we are upset too? We all love Dadabhai dearly. After Ma, he is our guardian."

"Shrirupa, are you sure it was Bikram who provided the water? Did Mrs. Deb take it directly from him?"

"Yes, I'm absolutely sure of that. She was desperate for water at that moment."

"Why did she eat such rich and spicy food, didn't she have dietary restrictions?"

"She followed a strict diet, but on a vacation, she indulged at times. She wasn't supposed to have rich food like Rajma or Kali Dal, but occasionally, it was alright doctor said. She didn't like spicy food as such. Of course, you can't expect hotel food to be bland."

"But she liked chilies, isn't it?"

"No! She couldn't tolerate hot spices. At home we only use whole green chili in cooking. Why are you asking all this Meghna di?"

"It's nothing, just a passing thought." Meghna smiled and took her leave, dragging Aditi along.

***

Aditi and Meghna reached the police station after breakfast. Aditi wanted to meet Bikram, so they decided to talk to SI Shridhar for permission. SP Kannan's jeep arrived there at the same time; he noticed the duo and greeted them. As they went inside, Aditi put in her request to Kannan. This time he was sympathetic towards her and instructed Shridhar to facilitate the meeting.

"Is your book in English, Madam?" Kannan addressed Meghna, as she was waiting in his cabin, while Aditi went to meet Bikram.

"Yes, if you're interested, I can give you the Kindle link," she shyly answered.

"Please do. I would love to read about the lazy police officer." He had a mischievous smile on his face. Meghna blushed at that.

"Have you taken fingerprints from the water glass, Sir?" She asked hesitatingly.

"We do fingerprint imaging of everything in a crime scene. Here too we did that for all the items on the table. Why do you ask?"

"Did you match it, Sir?"

"We have sent Bikram's sample. There are three types of prints on the glass. Understandably, two are of Bikram and the deceased, while the other could be from the waiter who kept it on the counter."

"The other fingerprint should be Shrirupa's, Sir. She brought food and water to Bikram's table. Could you match it please? The waiters usually wear gloves while manning the buffet counters." Kannan frowned at that, but he nodded in agreement.

"Yes, it's there in the statements too; I shouldn't have missed that point." He muttered.

"I will send Shridhar to take samples of fingerprints from all the three ladies who were present at the crime scene. Thank you, Madam." He gave a broad smile to Meghna.

"Send me the link of your book," he reminded her, as Aditi came back and the pair took their leave.

***

"What did Bikram say?" Meghna asked Aditi on their way back.

"At first he refused to talk and then told me to forget him and return to Kolkata."

"That's quite sensible, but made an opposite impact, I suppose? What did you say in reply?"

"What could I have said?" Aditi choked.

"Why, you should have said I will ruin my career and life for you and will stay in Hampi forever, if the need be; even if that means my poor friend will lose her job and maybe her husband too!" Meghna teased.

"You're impossible!" Aditi scolded her friend but understood the humour.

"Madam lets go for some good Chinese food to celebrate," Maruti remarked from the front seat of his autorickshaw.

"What's there to celebrate, Maruti? Aditi Ma'am is very sad, can't you see that?"

"But you said, you may stay here permanently; it demands celebration!" Hegrinned.

"Maruti, you too!" Aditi broke into a smile at that.

***

True to his word, Kannan sent his team immediately to the hotel to collect fingerprint samples.

It was afternoon, Meghna felt claustrophobic in the hotel room; Aditi refused to step out after returning from the police station. They even ordered lunch from room service. So, Meghna decided to go out on her own to get some fresh air; she now realised the depth of Aditi's emotion. It saddened her to see that the strong girl had become this affected by a man she hardly knew.

"Madam, can I talk to you for a minute?" It was Subhash, the other Bengali waiter. He approached Meghna, as she was coming out of her room. She was surprised to see him at the doorstep.

"What is it Subhash, do you want to come in?"

"No, I can talk here in the passage, it isn't that important."

"Yes, tell me!"

"It is actually quite trivial, may not be worth mentioning."

"If it is something related to the murder, any little information could be of great use. A man's life is at stake Subhash, we don't want an innocent man to be convicted."

He was about to speak when Meghna's mobile rang; it was SP Kannan. "I am reaching the hotel, could you please come to the office there?"

"Madam, you are busy, I shall come some other time," Subhash remarked after the phone call.

"You come with me, narrate your account in front of the SP."

"No Madam, I don't want to go there, I told you it's actually not that important." He was uncomfortable about interacting with the police.

"Subhash look at me; I am assuring that nothing will happen to you in case the information is worthless. Even if you talk to me in private, I will narrate your account to the SP and he will call you to take your statement. Don't worry, he is a good man." After much persuasion, Meghna convinced him and they headed for the office. Kannan was already there when they reached. Meghna asked Subhash to wait outside and then entered the room.

"I have matched the fingerprints; two were of Bikram and Mrs. Deb as anticipated; but the third one didn't match Shrirupa's."

"How is that possible, Sir?" Meghna was disappointed since much of the case depended on this finding.

"Subhash, one of the hotel staff is waiting outside, he wants to say something; you better listen to him, Sir," she gathered herself from the initial shock and remarked.

Subhash was called in and offered a seat; Kannan spoke to him informally; it was to boost the man's morale Meghnaunderstood.

"I was at the dessert counter; Mr. Bikram's table was straight ahead in my line of view. Uma, the attendant, took a bowl of custard from the counter and went to Bikram Sir's table; she had a glass of water in her hand too, probably meant for the old lady. She put the glass down right beside the glass of water on the table and then offered the bowl to Bikram Sir. While leaving the table she picked up the other glass. At that time, I thought it was a harmless mistake. Now that I hear about poison in the glass and Bikram Sir's arrest in that relation, it doesn't seem that normal anymore."

"Are you sure about this?" Meghna was confused.

"He's correct; the third fingerprint on the glass matched Uma's," Kannan declared. Meghna's face brightened up at that.

"Sir, please call another staff member, named Bibek. I think he can provide us with the missing clue."

Subhash got activated at that and called up Bibek, who came immediately to the office.

"Bibek, you mentioned Mrs. Deb took too much chili in her food. Why did you say so?" Meghna asked him as soon as he arrived.

"I saw Uma mixing a lot of chili flakes in the rajma she took for the old lady on that day," Bibek answered confidently.

"I told you, Sir; the rajma has a connection with the murder!" Meghna exclaimed.

"I get your point now, Madam; she put cocaine in the glass at the water table, which is unmanned, and exchanged it tactfully with Bikram's. Afterwards, the chili in the rajma would ensure that Mrs. Deb would require water urgently. Then, she must have broken the glass for the lady purposely, so that Bikram offered his. It was Uma who murdered the old lady!"

"And also incriminated Bikram at the same time," Meghna added.

Uma was taken into custody immediately; Bikram would be released late in the evening, Kannan assured.

"Good that the case has been solved within 24 hours of his arrest; we haven't yet made any charge-sheet against him," he remarked smilingly.

***

"What was her motive, Meghna?" Aditi asked during dinner that evening. Meghna, Aditi and Maruti had gone to a Chinese restaurant to celebrate. It was their last evening in Hampi; Meghna had already booked tickets for the train to Bangalore for next evening.

"It was more to punish Bikram than to kill the old lady, I feel."

"Why would she do so? She cared for Bikram I thought!"

"She cared for him, probably assumed he had same feelings towards her. She understood her mistake as soon as they reached this place and Bikram fell for you, head over heel. It's a crime of passion and planned on impulse."

"She was very clever with her plan, Madam!" Maruti remarked.

"People who struggle for their existence for too long, get humiliated and manipulated time and again, sometimes become cunning and manipulative themselves. She had the nerve to commit such a crime too. There was a great risk at many points; getting noticed while stealing the cocaine or mixing it with water and then exchanging the water glass. She could have been caught; yet took her chance."

***

She was sitting at the corner of the ladies' cell alone, head bent down, a bunch of disheveled locks hid her face from view. Bikram went ahead to talk to her before leaving the police station.

"Uma!" She stirred at that soft address, it always thrilled her whenever he took her name in that tone.

"Why did you do it, Uma? Look at the mess you are in now!" She looked up; her eyes swelled with tears.

"My life had always been a mess Bikram da; you were my onlyhope."

"If I was a disappointment, why didn't you tell me that? What made you take such an extreme step?" Bikram was exasperated.

"She always treated my mother like a nuisance; never made me forget I am a paid attendant; for that matter everyone in a position of power has always bullied me, the nursing home matron, agency head, your family members, everyone. I thought you were different; sensitive, respectful, you cared for me."

"I do, Uma, I genuinely care for you, that is why I am here!"

"No, you don't; I was a paid staff member for you too, not worthy of your love."

"Uma, I always treated you as a cousin; you are a cousin!"

"Don't give me that excuse, you are not to a blood relation to Masi." There was bitterness in her voice.

"Oh yes, I have come to know that lately. I am like those epiphytes that grow on the mother tree, but never become a part of it." There was something in his voice that troubled her. She kept looking at his face for a long moment.

"I am sorry Bikram da, I'm sorry for everything." She broke down at his feetsuddenly.

"I shall arrange for a lawyer for you, Uma. Stay safe." Bikram departed at that.

***

The next afternoon, Aditi was completing the checkout formalities at the hotel reception; Meghna stood by at theporch, as Maruti was engaged in loading the luggage in his auto-rikshaw.

"I will miss you, Maruti," she remarked, her voice soft with emotion.

"Can I call you, Didi?" He looked at her earnestly, those large eyes carried an innocent charm.

"Yes, of course!"

"When will you come again, Didi?"

"Maybe with your Jijaji soon; keep in touch, brother." Her eyes were moist; she didn't try to hide it.

Bikram accompanied them to the railway station; Meghna stood aside on the platform, giving the couple some privacy. The train arrived in a while; it was time to board at last.

"Does the commoner win the princess finally?"Bikram whispered.

"I think so!" Aditi gave her sweetest smile, while boarding the train.

"It was quite an experience!"She remarked dreamily, as they settled down in the compartment.

"With a happy ending, isn't it?" Meghna winked and then her phone rang.

"Madam, I read your book last night; let me give some honest feedback. You are smarter than your detective."The call ended with that and Meghna laughed heartily.

*** THE END ***

www.ingramcontent.com/pod-product-compliance
Lightning Source LLC
LaVergne TN
LVHW091155180726
843490LV00007B/2446